WOULD YOU RATHER

BOOK FOR KIDS

Sunny Panda
Publishing

ISBN - 9781072630579

WOULD YOU RATHER...

HAVE TO SING WHEN INTRODUCING YOURSELF TO SOMEONE NEW

~OR~

HAVE TO BREAK INTO DANCE FOR 3 MINUTES?

HAVE A FLYING MAGIC CARPET

~OR~

A PET TIGER?

WOULD YOU RATHER...

NEVER BE ABLE TO PLAY
VIDEO GAMES AGAIN

~OR~

NEVER BE ABLE TO EAT
CANDY AGAIN?

BE FACE TO FACE WITH A DRAGON

SWIM WITH SHARKS
FOR 10 MINUTES?

WOULD YOU RATHER...

HAVE A PIG
NOSE

~OR~

HAVE DOG EARS AND TONGUE?

DISCOVER BURIED TREASURE

NEVER HAVE TO DO HOMEWORK
EVER AGAIN?

WOULD YOU RATHER...

NEVER WATCH A MOVIE AGAIN

~OR~

NEVER LISTEN TO MUSIC AGAIN?

GO TO AN AMUSEMENT PARK
WHENEVER YOU WANT

~OR~

GO TO THE BEACH
WHENEVER YOU WANT?

WOULD YOU RATHER...

GET STUNG BY A BEE EVERY DAY
FOR
THE REST OF YOUR LIFE
~OR~
BURP UNCONTROLLABLY?

HAVE A MOVIE
THEATHER
IN YOUR HOUSE
~OR~

HAVE A WATER SLIDE?

WOULD YOU RATHER...

HAVE TO READ A
BOOK EVERY DAY

EAT YOUR LEAST FAVORITE
FOOD AT EVERY MEAL?

BE ABLE TO READ MINDS

~OR~

MOVE OBJECTS WITH YOUR MIND?

WOULD YOU RATHER...

LIVE IN A HOT AIR

BALLOON

~OR~

LIVE IN A ROW BOAT?

NEVER FEEL PAIN AGAIN

~OR~

HAVE ANY FOOD YOU

WANT INSTANTLY?

WOULD YOU RATHER...

BE A PROFESSIONAL

SURFER

~OR~

BE A ROCKSTAR?

WEAR SHORTS AND FLIP

FLIPS IN THE SNOW

~OR~

WEAR A SWEATSUIT IN

HUMID HEAT?

WOULD YOU RATHER...

BE ABLE TO SPEAK ANY LANGUAGE

~OR~

BE ABLE TO PLAY ANY INSTRUMENT?

NOT PLAY WITH FRIENDS
FOR A MONTH

~OR~

EAT AN EARTHWORM EVERY DAY
FOR A WHOLE YEAR?

WOULD YOU RATHER...

HAVE ANY SUPERPOWER YOU WANT AT YOUR COMMAND

~OR~

NEVER HAVE TO WORK A DAY IN YOUR LIFE?

LIVE WHERE IT NEVER STOPS RAINING

~OR~

LIVE IN THE HOT AND DRY DESERT?

WOULD YOU RATHER...

BE THE WORLD'S BEST SKATEBOARDER

~OR~

COME UP WITH A SUPER COOL INVENTION?

BE ALLOWED TO STAY UP
AS LATE AS YOU WANT

~OR~

EAT WHATEVER YOU WANT?

WOULD YOU RATHER...

LIVE IN A TINY HOUSE IN THE CITY

~OR~

LIVE IN A BIG HOUSE IN
THE MIDDLE OF NOWHERE?

ALWAYS KNOW WHEN SOMEONE IS LYING

~OR~

HAVE A PHOTOGRAPHIC MEMORY?

WOULD YOU RATHER...

GIVE A SPEECH IN FRONT
OF THOUSANDS OF PEOPLE

~OR~

GO SKYDIVING?

GET ANY CAR YOU WANT

~OR~

OWN A HELICOPTER?

WOULD YOU RATHER...

ONLY BE ABLE TO TAKE
A SHOWER ONCE A WEEK

~OR~

ONLY BE ABLE TO BRUSH
YOUR TEETH ONCE A WEEK?

BE A LEGENDARY BREAKDANCER

~OR~

BE THE FASTEST RUNNER ALIVE?

WOULD YOU RATHER...

HAVE TO LISTEN TO A CAR ALARM

FOR 5 MINUTES EVERY HOUR

~OR~

FOR 2 HOURS STRAIGHT EVERY WEEK?

HAVE AN ENORMOUS AND

DECKED OUT TREEHOUSE

~OR~

HAVE A GIANT SWIMMING POOL

WITH WATER SLIDES AND

DIVING BOARDS?

WOULD YOU RATHER...

HAVE A PET DOLPHIN

HAVE A PET MONKEY?

MOVE TO A NEW TOWN EVERY YEAR

~OR~

NEVER LEAVE YOUR HOMETOWN,
EVEN FOR VACATION?

WOULD YOU RATHER...

DISCOVER SOMETHING THAT WILL
MAKE THE HISTORY BOOKS

~OR~

BE BEST FRIENDS WITH ANY
FAMOUS PERSON YOU PICK?

HAVE TO WEAR THE SAME
OUTFIT EVERY DAY

~OR~

HAVE TO EAT THE SAME
THING EVERY DAY?

WOULD YOU RATHER...

GET UNLIMITED MOVIE TICKETS

~OR~

GO TO AN AMUSEMENT PARK
EVERY MONTH?

HAVE A DENTIST
APPOINTMENT ONCE A WEEK

~OR~

GET A SHOT ONCE A WEEK?

WOULD YOU RATHER...

NEVER FEEL FEAR AGAIN

NEVER FEEL PAIN AGAIN?

VACATION ANY PLACE
YOU CHOOSE

SKIP ONE MONTH OF SCHOOL?

WOULD YOU RATHER...

BE FORCED TO SCREAM ANYTIME
SOMEONE SAYS YOUR NAME

~**OR**~

HAVE CHRONIC AND
INVOLUNTARY HICCUPS?

SLEEP ON THE FLOOR EVERY NIGHT

~**OR**~

SLEEP IN A TREE TWICE A WEEK?

WOULD YOU RATHER...

NEVER GET SICK AGAIN

~OR~

GET NEW CLOTHES EVERY WEEK?

GIVE UP SWEETS FOR A YEAR

~OR~

NOT WATCH TV FOR A YEAR?

WOULD YOU RATHER...

HAVE AS MANY PETS
AS YOU WANT

~OR~

STAY UP LATE EVERY NIGHT?

HAVE A TRAMPOLINE PARK
IN YOUR BACKYARD

~OR~

HAVE A HOT TUB IN YOUR BEDROOM?

WOULD YOU RATHER...

GO TO SCHOOL FOR TWO **REALLY**

LONG DAYS PER WEEK

~**OR**~

KEEP WITH YOUR

NORMAL SCHOOL SCHEDULE?

BE AN AMAZING GUITAR PLAYER

~**OR**~

BE AN AMAZING

BASKETBALL PLAYER?

WOULD YOU RATHER...

CLIMB MOUNT EVEREST

~OR~

BE STUCK SWIMMING IN THE MIDDLE
OF THE OCEAN FOR 12 HOURS?

BE EXTREMELY CLUTSY

~OR~

BE EXTREMELY GASSY?

WOULD YOU RATHER...

NEVER FEEL ANNOYED EVER AGAIN

NEVER FEEL HUNGRY EVER AGAIN?

GO BUNGEE JUMPING

GO ROCK CLIMBING?

WOULD YOU RATHER...

HAVE THREE ARMS

~OR~

A TAIL AND ANIMAL EARS?

TRAVEL TO ANYWHERE IN THE WORLD
ONCE A MONTH

ALWAYS HAVE A FOUR DAY WEEKEND?

WOULD YOU RATHER...

BE IN A SMALL SPACE WITH
LOTS OF SPIDERS
~OR~
BE IN A CAGE WITH A FEW SNAKES?

BE FORCED TO RUN A
MILE EVERY DAY?
~OR~
RUN 7 MILES ONCE A WEEK?

WOULD YOU RATHER...

SPEND 4 HOURS IN YOUR
FAVORITE CLASS
~OR~
SPEND 2 HOURS IN YOUR
LEAST FAVORITE CLASS?

NEVER BE ABLE TO HAVE
YOUR OWN PHONE
~OR~
NEVER BE ABLE TO HAVE YOUR OWN CAR?

WOULD YOU RATHER...

LOSE YOUR SENSE OF SMELL

LOSE YOU SENSE OF TOUCH?

BE LOST IN NEW YORK CITY
FOR A DAY BY YOURSELF?

BE HOME ALONE FOR A WEEK?

WOULD YOU RATHER...

NEVER BE BORED

~OR~

NEVER BE TIRED?

HAVE TO WALK TO SCHOOL EVERY DAY

~OR~

DO TWICE AS MUCH
HOMEWORK EVERY NIGHT?

WOULD YOU RATHER...

BE AN INCREDIBLE ARTIST

AN INCREDIBLE ATHLETE?

HAVE ITCHY MOSQUITO
BITES ALL OVER YOUR BODY

EAT A BOWL OF WORMS?

WOULD YOU RATHER...

BE ALLOWED TO DO
WHATEVER YOU WANT

~OR~

HAVE THE ABILITY TO
FLY ONE HOUR A WEEK?

WAKE UP AN HOUR EARLIER
EVERY MORNING

~OR~

GO TO BED AN HOUR EARLIER
EVERY NIGHT?

WOULD YOU RATHER...

BE EXTREMELY STRONG

BE EXTREMELY FAST?

HAVE A RAT SNEAK
INTO YOUR ROOM

HAVE A DOZEN SPIDERS SNEAK IN?

WOULD YOU RATHER...

CLEAN THE ENTIRE HOUSE

~OR~

CLEAN THE TOILET
WITH A TOOTHBRUSH?

GO TO A TRAMPOLINE PARK

~OR~

A WATER PARK?

WOULD YOU RATHER...

MEET A CELEBRITY MUSICIAN

~OR~

A MOVIE STAR?

BATHE IN A SINK FOR A MONTH

~OR~

A DUCK POND FOR A WEEK?

WOULD YOU RATHER...

HOLD A TARANTULA

A HISSING MADAGASCAR
COCKROACH?

BE A TRAVELING PHOTOGRAPHER

A PROFESSIONAL DANCER?

WOULD YOU RATHER...

HAVE A STOMACH ACHE

 ~OR~

HAVE A REALLY BAD HEADACHE?

SPEND THE DAY AT THE BEACH

 ~OR~

WATCH TWO MOVIES ON
A SCHOOL NIGHT?

WOULD YOU RATHER...

EAT DOG FOOD

~OR~

GET A SPLINTER?

BE ABLE TO TURN INVISIBLE

~OR~

NOT HAVE ANY HOMEWORK

FOR A YEAR?

WOULD YOU RATHER...

WEAR YOUR SHOES ON THE WRONG FEET

~OR~

WEAR GLOVES 24/7?

SWIM IN A TANK
WITH JELLYFISH

~OR~

BE LOCKED IN A SMALL
ROOM WITH SCORPIONS

WOULD YOU RATHER...

HAVE SUPER LONG
NAILS YOU CAN'T CUT

~OR~

HAVE AN EXTRA TOE ON BOTH FEET?

DRINK A GLASS OF LIQUID SOAP

~OR~

SHOVEL COW POOP FOR
30 MINUTES WITHOUT A MASK?

WOULD YOU RATHER...

GET PAID TO DO CHORES

NOT HAVE TO DO ANY CHORES?

WIN A TRIP TO ANYWHERE
IN THE WORLD

WIN $1,000?

WOULD YOU RATHER...

HAVE TO CLIMB A
REALLY TALL TREE

SWIM FAR OUT INTO THE OCEAN?

NOT LEAVE YOUR ROOM FOR A MONTH

~OR~

HAVE TO WALK EVERYWHERE
BAREFOOT FOR A MONTH?

WOULD YOU RATHER...

WASH DISHES FOR 3 HOURS

CLEAN TOILETS FOR 1 HOUR?

HAVE UNLIMITED ICECREAM

UNLIMITED PIZZA?

WOULD YOU RATHER...

BE ABLE TO TALK TO ANIMALS

~OR~

BE THE STRONGEST PERSON ALIVE?

PARACHUTE JUMP INTO
THE GRAND CANYON

~OR~

WRESTLE AN ALLIGATOR?

WOULD YOU RATHER...

NEVER NEED TO GO TO THE BATHROOM

NEVER NEED TO SLEEP?

BE A DOCTOR

AN ASTRONAUT?

WOULD YOU RATHER...

BE ABLE TO DO TEN
BACKFLIPS IN A ROW

WALKING HANDSTANDS?

ACCIDENTALLY FART IN CLASS

GET IN TROUBLE WITH YOUR TEACHER

WOULD YOU RATHER...

BE THE TALLEST PERSON IN YOUR FAMILY

~OR~

THE SHORTEST PERSON IN YOUR FAMILY?

HAVE 100 GOOD FRIENDS

~OR~

HAVE 10 AMAZING FRIENDS?

WOULD YOU RATHER...

THERE WERE NO BUGS
IN THE WORLD

~OR~

THERE WAS NO SUCH
THING AS CHORES?

TIME MACHINES EXISTED

~OR~

TELEPORTATION WAS POSSIBLE?

WOULD YOU RATHER...

IF TIME MACHINES DID EXIST...

GO INTO THE PAST

~OR~

INTO THE FUTURE?

HAVE EYES THAT FILLED
UP HALF YOUR FACE

~OR~

HAVE A MOUTH THAT FILLS
UP HALF YOUR FACE?

WOULD YOU RATHER...

LIVE ALONE IN A VERY SMALL HOUSE

~OR~

LIVE WITH 50 PEOPLE
IN A VERY LARGE HOUSE?

LISTEN TO NAILS ON A CHALKBOARD

~OR~

A FIRETRUCK SIREN?

WOULD YOU RATHER...

BE AN ADULT

~OR~

BE A KID FOREVER?

BE EXTREMELY SMART

~OR~

BE EXTREMELY TALENTED?

WOULD YOU RATHER...

HAVE REALLY LARGE HANDS

VERY SMALL FEET?

BE ABLE TO PREDICT THE FUTURE

BE ABLE TO KNOW WHAT
SOMEONE IS THINKING?

WOULD YOU RATHER...

NEVER BE ABLE TO WEAR RED AGAIN

NEVER BE ABLE TO WEAR BLUE AGAIN?

BE IN A HOUSE WITH A CLOSEBY TORNADO

A CLOSEBY HURRICANE?

WOULD YOU RATHER...

NOT HAVE A SENSE OF TASTE

ONLY SEE IN BLACK AND WHITE?

HAVE A FULL TIME PERSONAL CHEF

~OR~

A FULL TIME HOUSECLEANER?

WOULD YOU RATHER...

BE EXTREMELY FORGETFUL

BE EXTREMELY CLUMSY?

BE STRANDED ON AN ISLAND
WITH YOUR BEST FRIEND
FOR 6 MONTHS

~OR~

BE GROUNDED TO YOUR ROOM
ALONE FOR A YEAR?

WOULD YOU RATHER...

BE LIMITED TO PEANUT
BUTTER AND WATER

~OR~

CRACKERS AND MILK?

HAVE TO WALK ON STILTS
EVERYWHERE YOU GO

~OR~

HAVE TO CRAWL ON ALL FOURS?

WOULD YOU RATHER...

HAVE 10 DOGS

HAVE 10 CATS?

BE IMMUNE TO EVERY
ILLNESS IN THE WORLD

NEVER FEEL FEAR?

WOULD YOU RATHER...

HAVE UNCONTROLLABLE SCREAMING

 ~OR~

HAVE UNCONTROLLABLE CRYING?

NOT GET ENOUGH SLEEP

~OR~

NOT GET ENOUGH FOOD?

WOULD YOU RATHER...

HAVE ANY TOY/GADGET YOU CAN IMAGINE

~OR~

TRAVEL ANYWHERE YOU WANT?

FIND A UNICORN

~OR~

FIND A LIVING DINOSAUR?

WOULD YOU RATHER...

LOSE YOUR ABILITY TO
SPEAK FOR A YEAR

~OR~

HAVE TO SAY EVERYTHING
YOU'RE THINKING FOR 6 MONTHS?

HAVE YOUR GRANDPARENT'S
HAIRSTYLE

~OR~

THEIR WARDROBE?

WOULD YOU RATHER...

EAT NOTHING BUT CATFOOD FOR A DAY

~OR~

HAVE TO SCOOP THEIR LITTERBOX BARE HANDED FOR A WEEK

BE A STAND UP COMEDIAN

~OR~

BE A CHEF?

WOULD YOU RATHER...

RUN UPHILL FOR 30 MINUTES

~OR~

RUN DOWNHILL FOR 1 HOUR?

LIVE IN THE CITY

~OR~

OR THE COUNTRY?

WOULD YOU RATHER...

BE THE WORST PLAYER ON A WINNING TEAM

~OR~

BE THE BEST PLAYER ON A LOSING TEAM?

OWN YOUR OWN PLANE

~OR~

OWN YOUR OWN BOAT?

WOULD YOU RATHER...

MEET A FICTIONAL CHARACTER
LIKE PETER PAN

~OR~

A REAL PERSON FROM THE PAST
LIKE ABRAHAM LINCOLN?

HAVE A HEAD THREE TIMES AS BIG

~OR~

THREE TIMES AS SMALL?

WOULD YOU RATHER...

ALWAYS HAVE TO ENTER A ROOM

WALKING BACKWARDS

~OR~

ALWAYS HAVE TO ENTER

HYSTERICALLY LAUGHING?

LIVE IN OUTER SPACE

UNDER THE OCEAN?

WOULD YOU RATHER...

BE A BIRD

~OR~

A CHEETAH?

LIVE ON CHEETOS

~OR~

DORITOS?

WOULD YOU RATHER...

HAVE A ROOM FULL OF CRICKETS

~OR~

JUST A FEW COCKROACHES?

BE ABLE TO TRY A DIFFERENT
HAIRSTYLE/COLOR EVERY DAY

~OR~

HAVE A NEW OUTFIT EVERY DAY

WOULD YOU RATHER...

BE REALLY GOOD AT SINGING

~OR~

REALLY GOOD AT DANCING?

GO PARASAILING

~OR~

WATER SKIING?

WOULD YOU RATHER...

HAVE ONE EXTRA EYE ON YOUR FACE

~OR~

HAVE FOUR EARS?

EAT AT HOME, BUT GO TO YOUR
FAVORITE RESTURAUNT ONCE A MONTH

GO TO A GOOD, NOT GREAT,
RESTURAUNT EVERY NIGHT?

WOULD YOU RATHER...

BE PRETTY GOOD AT EVERYTHING

~OR~

AMAZING AT A COUPLE THINGS?

BE ABLE TO BREATHE UNDERWATER

~OR~

BE ABLE TO SEE THROUGH THINGS?

WOULD YOU RATHER...

BE A WIZARD

~OR~

A DRAGON?

NEVER BE COLD

NEVER BE HOT?

WOULD YOU RATHER...

PLAY PIANO REALLY WELL

PLAY GUITAR REALLY WELL?

HAVE AN EXTRA LONG SUMMER

~OR~

HAVE SCHOOL DAYS BE SHORTER?

WOULD YOU RATHER...

JUMP INTO A DUMPSTER FULL OF

ICE FOR 1 MINUTE

~OR~

A DUMPSTER FULL OF PB AND JELLY

FOR 5 MINUTES?

NEVER HAVE TO SHOWER AGAIN

~OR~

NEVER HAVE TO SLEEP AGAIN?

WOULD YOU RATHER...

BE A FAMOUS MUSICIAN

~OR~

AN ACCOMPLISHED ATHLETE?

HAVE A GO-CART TRACK IN
YOUR BACKYARD
~OR~
HAVE A ROCK CLIMBING SET-UP?

WOULD YOU RATHER...

HAVE WOLVERINE CLAWS

HAVE VAMPIRE TEETH?

LIVE NEXT DOOR TO A ZOO

LIVE NEXT TO AN
AMUSEMENT PARK?

WOULD YOU RATHER...

BE FORCED TO WEAR
DIRTY CLOTHES FOR A WEEK

~OR~

NOT BE ALLOWED TO
BRUSH YOUR HAIR?

HAVE ELF EARS

~OR~

OR A DOG TAIL?

WOULD YOU RATHER...

GIVE UP FURNITURE FOR 6 MONTHS

OR YOUR FAVORITE FOOD FOR A YEAR?

WALK FOR 2 HOURS
EVERY DAY

~OR~

CLEAN THE HOUSE
FOR AN HOUR EVERY DAY?

WOULD YOU RATHER...

BE FORCED TO SHAVE YOUR HEAD

BE FORCED TO GROW YOUR
HAIR DOWN TO YOUR FEET?

NOT HAVE A SUNNY DAY FOR A YEAR

NOT PLAY VIDEO GAMES FOR A YEAR?

WOULD YOU RATHER...

WALK BAREFOOT EVERYWHERE

WEAR GIANT BOOTS EVERYWHERE?

MEET A MERMAID

MEET AN ELF?

WOULD YOU RATHER...

GO WITHOUT YOUR BEST
FRIEND FOR 6 MONTHS

HAVE IT SNOW EVERY DAY
FOR AN ENTIRE YEAR?

HAVE A REALLY GIANT HEAD

HAVE SUPER BIG FEET?

WOULD YOU RATHER...

EAT SPAGHETTI EVERY NIGHT FOR DINNER

~OR~

ONLY BE ALLOWED TO DRINK WATER
AND NOTHING ELSE?

LIVE THE SAME GREAT DAY
OVER AND OVER FOR A YEAR

~OR~

LIVE A DIFFERENT, BUT ONLY OKAY
DAY FOR A YEAR?

WOULD YOU RATHER...

HAVE A BRAND NEW COMPUTER
AND PHONE RIGHT NOW

~OR~

HAVE A BRAND NEW CAR FOR
WHEN YOU TURN 16?

BE REALLY SMART

BE REALLY GOOD AT SPORTS?

WOULD YOU RATHER...

SLEEP IN THE WOODS BY
YOURSELF ONCE A WEEK

~OR~

SLEEP ON THE FLOOR OF YOUR
BEDROOM EVERY NIGHT?

GO ON A ROLLERCOASTER
THAT **REALLY** SCARES YOU

~OR~

RUN A MARATHON?

WOULD YOU RATHER...

SHAVE YOUR HEAD FOR 6 MONTHS

GROW YOUR TOENAILS OUT
FOR 6 MONTHS?

LIVE IN A SHACK ON THE BEACH

~OR~

LIVE IN A MANSION IN
THE MIDDLE OF NOWHERE?

WOULD YOU RATHER...

NOT BE ALLOWED TO DRIVE
WHEN YOU GET OLDER

~OR~

HAVE TO WORK EVERY DAY OF THE WEEK
WITHOUT A DAY OFF?

BE A SUPERHERO

~OR~

OWN A UNICORN?

WOULD YOU RATHER...

STAND ON TOP OF A SKYSCRAPER
WITHOUT SUPPORT
~OR~
SIT ON A FLOATIE IN THE
MIDDLE OF THE OCEAN?

SLEEP WITH NO BLANKETS IN THE WINTER
AND THE AIR CONDITIONER ON
~OR~
UNDER 10 BLANKETS DURING
THE HUMID SUMMER?

WOULD YOU RATHER...

HAVE TO DRINK A GIANT BUCKET OF
WATER EVERY DAY

~OR~

HAVE TO RUN THREE MILES EVERY DAY?

HAVE CHICKEN POX FOR
THE REST OF YOUR LIFE

~OR~

HAVE A COLD FOR HALF
OF EVERY MONTH?

WOULD YOU RATHER...

BE A TEACHER

~OR~

BE A LANDSCAPER?

HAVE A BIRD NEST IN YOUR HAIR

~OR~

ALWAYS SMELL LIKE A SKUNK?

WOULD YOU RATHER...

HAVE YOUR FEET ALWAYS FEEL

LIKE THEY'RE ASLEEP

~OR~

STUB A TOE REALLY BAD ONCE

AN HOUR?

NEVER BE ABLE TO SIT

DOWN AGAIN

~OR~

HAVE TO SLEEP SITTING

UP FOREVER?

WOULD YOU RATHER...

BE FORCED TO READ THE ENTIRE
NEWSPAPER EVERY MORNING

HAVE TO WALK TO
AND FROM SCHOOL?

HAVE LICE FOR A YEAR

HAVE A COLD FOR A YEAR?

WOULD YOU RATHER...

STAND OUT

BLEND IN?

GO WITHOUT YOUR TOOTHBRUSH

YOUR HAIRBRUSH?

WOULD YOU RATHER...

HAVE A GIANT FUZZY UNIBROW

 ~OR~

SUPER HAIRY FEET?

JUMP INTO A FREEZING COLD STREAM

~OR~

GO CLIFF JUMPING OFF
A REALLY HIGH SPOT?

WOULD YOU RATHER...

HAVE TO GO TO THE
GROCERY STORE EVERY DAY

~OR~

HAVE TO DO THE DISHES EVERY DAY?

WORK AT A SUPER
BUSY COFFEE SHOP

~OR~

WORK AT A QUIET LIBRARY?

WOULD YOU RATHER...

WAKE UP EARLIER AND
GET OUT OF SCHOOL EARLY

~OR~

SLEEP IN LATER AND
GET OUT OF SCHOOL LATER?

GET A PRESENT ONCE A
MONTH FOR A YEAR

~OR~

GET A DOZEN PRESENTS ONCE A YEAR?

WOULD YOU RATHER...

FACE YOUR BIGGEST FEAR

~OR~

WALK ACROSS HOT COALS?

GO ICE SKATING

~OR~

GO ROLLER BLADING?

WOULD YOU RATHER...

HAVE THE ABILITY TO SHAPE SHIFT

~OR~

INSTANTLY TELEPORT?

LOSE A TARANTULA
IN YOUR ROOM

~OR~

LOSE A DOZEN MICE?

WOULD YOU RATHER...

BE RICH AND FAMOUS

~OR~

HAVE SUPERPOWERS,
BUT NOBODY KNOWS IT?

LIVE IN A GIANT
CHOCOLATE FACTORY

~OR~

LIVE AT A CARNIVAL?

WOULD YOU RATHER...

HAVE TONS OF FRIENDS

HAVE TONS OF TOYS AND GADGETS?

BE IN A CEMETARY
AT NIGHT WITH YOUR FRIEND

BE HOME ALONE FOR A WEEK?

WOULD YOU RATHER...

STAR IN A MOVIE

~OR~

HAVE UNLIMITED GIFT CARDS AT THE MALL?

HAVE A POOL FULL OF JELLO

~OR~

HAVE A TREE FORT WITH
ROPE SWINGS NEXT TO A POND?

THE END.